Chris Owen started to write about
Hairy Mole whilst living in a tent in
the hills of Figline Valdarno,
Tuscany, Italy.

After travelling through Asia and
teaching in Taiwan, he now lives by
the sea in sunny Hove, East Sussex.

If you'd like to contact Chris, then
details are available on the Hairy
Mole website:

www.hairymolethepirate.co.uk

Also by Chris Owen:

Hairy Mole
and the
Precious
Islands

by

Chris Owen

Ransom

Hairy Mole and the Precious Islands

by Chris Owen
Illustrated by David Mostyn

Published by Ransom Publishing Ltd.
Radley House, 8 St. Cross Road, Winchester,
Hampshire SO23 9HX
www.ransom.co.uk

ISBN   978 184167 082 9
First published in 2008
This edition published 2013
Copyright © 2013 Ransom Publishing Ltd.

Text copyright © 2013 Chris Owen
Illustrations copyright © 2013 David Mostyn

Dedications

Many thanks to all the pirates who have enjoyed reading Hairy Mole's previous adventures. I hope you enjoy this offering.

Welcome to the world, Harry and George Oliver and Teseo Poma. Also a big yo-ho-ho to Harley and Luke Rouse.

Special thanks to Denno and his amazing eyebrows.

As always, love and peace to my family, especially Nikki, Mum and Dad and Ken and Penny.

May your love of jam and pickles never fade.

Chris Owen

One

Clint East Mole

"Eeeek!" thought Hairy Mole, as he examined the five cards splayed in his grubby hand.

The King of Hearts, sporting a particularly ginger mullet, beamed up at him.

The rest of the cards peeked from behind the King, gradually revealing themselves, as Hairy Mole's thumb forced them out of their hiding place: a two of Clubs, the six of Hearts, the four of Hearts and finally a second King, this time bearded and wearing what looked like a novelty apron: the King of Clubs.

"OK, OK, this is it, Moley my lad. One more go and you've got her, you've got her right where you want her." The pirate's brow furrowed in concentration as the thoughts entered his head.

Hairy Mole slammed the three non-picture cards down onto the table.

"Hit me!" he announced dramatically.

Three new cards were dealt into the clutches of Hairy Mole's warty fingers, and immediately they had their identities concealed behind the two Kings he already held in his hand.

Hairy Mole took great care not to reveal the cards' identities to his opponent. Carefully, using just his thumb and forefinger, the cards were teased into the open, introducing themselves one by one.

"Come on baby, papa needs a new pair of shoes." Hairy Mole had started to think to himself in the voice of Clint Eastwood, and he squinted his eyes into two tiny slits as the new cards began to emerge from their hiding place.

First, the six of Clubs.

"Noooooooooooooo!"

Clint cried in Hairy Mole's head.

This time, even more tentatively, he examined the remaining two cards.

Was that a crown? Was it, was it?

"Ooooh. Globbits!"

Clint screamed, as the arrogant-looking Jack of Diamonds gave Hairy Mole a little wink and sat laughing in his hand.

One card left to see. Could this be a King? Could Hairy Mole the Pirate be catapulted into poker heaven with three bearded members of the playing card royal family?

"Gently, gently, geeeently,"

Clint advised, as the big, dirty-nailed thumb

squeezed the final card out into the open.

"Whooooooooooop!" Clint squeaked with delight in a most unlike-Clint fashion.

Hairy Mole grinned with pleasure, showing off his black teeth, before quickly adopting a more nonchalant poker face.

He knew that he was sitting pretty, with the King of Hearts, the King of Clubs and, finally, the elusive King of Diamonds in his hand. Well, sitting as pretty as you can with a nose like a turnip and ears with more wax than all the candles in the Vatican.

"What have you got, Cat?" Hairy Mole placed his cards face-down on the table and stared at his opponent. He raised a hairy eyebrow and allowed the corners of his cracked lips to rise ever so slightly, in anticipation of winning the crown of best card-player in the kitchen.

"Come on, Milky Whiskers, let's see your paw."

Opposite Hairy Mole there came an indignant sigh and, after a quick scratch behind the ear and a stare that could have turned milk to ice-cream, T-towel the Cat finally spoke. "Two pair, my

filthy-nostrilled friend, two pair!"

T-towel raised an eyebrow and started to s m o o t h her whiskers back, as she looked at Hairy Mole squirming with delight in his chair.

T-towel began to turn her cards over one by one: the Ace of Clubs, the Ace of Diamonds ...

But before she could finish, Hairy Mole, unable to contain himself at the prospect of finally beating his feline opponent for the first time in history, flipped his own cards over and proudly declared himself **King of the Kitchen.**

Hairy Mole sat **beaming**, waiting for a reaction from his poker-faced opponent as sweat poured from his rosy-red cheeks and plopped onto the old oak table.

"Just out of interest, young T-towel, what were the other cards besides those two measly Aces?" Hairy Mole let out an almighty pirate laugh that he had been practising for weeks:

"Haaaaaaahaaaaaaaheeeeee heeeeehaaaaaaaaw!"

"Well, OK then, if you must know," smiled the cat, revelling in the moment.

"I had a pair of Aces, and ... oh look," T-towel flicked over another two cards with an outstretched claw, "another two Aces, making two pair. Or I suppose you could call it four deuces, baby.

Read 'em and weep!"

That is precisely what Hairy Mole did; he threw his hands onto the old oak table and wept like a leaking tap.

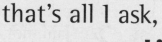

"Why me, why me? Please, let me beat her just once, that's all I ask, just once!"

Two

Room for a Little Guff?

Hairy Mole's mother was away for the weekend, and so the larder had been left full for any guests who may be passing by and in need of sustenance.

There were HUGE joints of ham, several large basted turkeys, six or seven jars of pickles and a vast quantity of jam, not to mention some very smelly cheese and a barrel full of bananas.

Hairy Mole was preparing dinner for six of his favourite friends.

He busied himself in the garden, pulling up bright orange carrots with green hairy tops. He

15

pulled up brown *dirty* potatoes, piling them into a potato mountain on the soft, green grass beside the vegetable patch.

Hairy Mole visited the larder again and returned with a huge basted turkey.

After rolling up his sleeves and washing his **filthy** hands, he stuck his arm up the turkey's bottom, right up to his elbow! T-towel the Cat sat watching with a look bordering on horror.

"Got 'em!" Hairy cried with delight, producing a juicy set of giblets from the turkey's backside, rather like a magician producing a bunch of flowers from a top hat.

"There you go, T-towel, you lucky old cat." The giblets landed s p l a t on T-towel's plate, as Hairy Mole manoeuvred the rest of the turkey into the oven, covered in lard and a sprinkling of herbs.

"You must be joking, fatty," thought T-towel to herself, and promptly stuck her nose in the air and headed for the back door in search of something slightly more appetising than a large bird's intestines.

It was just at that moment that there was a tap tap tap at the kitchen window-pane.

"Who could that be?" said Hairy to himself, looking at his genuine 'made to last' pirate pocket watch.

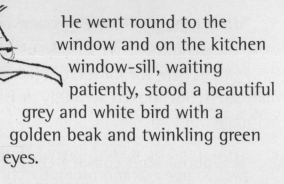

He went round to the window and on the kitchen window-sill, waiting patiently, stood a beautiful grey and white bird with a golden beak and twinkling green eyes.

The bird's feathers were sleek and soft, to help with flight. They were also sleek and soft because this was one c o o l seagull, and this c o o l seagull was never seen with an unruffled feather out of place.

"So, Toby the Seagull. What brings you tap, tapping on my kitchen window? You know, you're just in time for dinner, if you're interested!"

"Unfortunately, I haven't come here to taste the delights of Mrs Bulbous Mole's larder. I am here for far more serious matters!" Toby looked seriously at Hairy Mole before beginning.

"It is about your cousin Furry. Furry Mole. It appears that young Furry has got himself into a spot of bother."

Now, Furry Mole was quite a few years younger than Hairy, and he always seemed to be getting himself into some scrape or another. There was the time when he was two years old and he got his head stuck in a bowl full of jelly. There was the time when he was four years old and got stuck on top of the roof after chasing squirrels, much to Auntie Humongous' great distress.

And I won't even tell you what happened to the next door neighbour's rabbit. Suffice to say that it couldn't look at a ball of cotton wool without a lump appearing in its little throat.

After Toby had finished, Hairy Mole sat open-mouthed, baring his twitching epiglottis for the entire world to see. He was well and truly flabbergasted; in fact, he was well and truly blubbergasted. Come to think of it, he was well and truly flubberblubbergasted!

Just at that moment, there was a knock at the door. Hairy had completely forgotten the meal he was preparing, and as his guests arrived he continued to tut to himself as he welcomed them in and strained the vegetables.

First to arrive was a young scamp named Pickle the Pirate, who was sporting a rather fashionable pirate neckerchief.

"Hi Hairy, what's cooking?" Pickle sauntered into the kitchen before plopping himself down at the old oak kitchen table.

"More than vegetables, I can tell you, young Pickle. Just you wait until you hear what news Toby the Seagull has to offer." Hairy Mole had just sat himself down next to Pickle when there was another knock at the door.

"Two more urchins, is it? I think I can guess who we have here." As the door was opened, in bowled the twins, Crevice and Pit, rubbing their $ru_{mb}li_{ng}$ bellies with their oversized hands.

"What's cooking, Hairy Mole?"
"What's cooking, Hairy Mole?"
the twins cried out together.

"More than vegetables apparently!" Pickle called out from his place at the table.

Knock. Knock. Knock.

In the doorway stood a fearsome-looking pirate with large nostrils, hairy ears and the type of stubble that you could grate cheese on.

"Hello, Hairy." The pirate spoke in an absurdly high voice. "What's cooking?"

STAMP knock, STAMP knock. The pirate had only one real leg. The other, the left, was made of what looked like a cricket

21

bat. The sound of his wooden leg knocked on the stone kitchen floor.

"Ah, Mr Bogey, if it isn't yourself. Now, get useful and give me a hand with this dinner."

Squeak
Squeak

"It's the window!" pointed Pickle. As everyone turned, a large squidgy nose was slowly working its way down the length of the kitchen window.

"Door please, Pickle," asked Hairy Mole, as he tumbled the food onto the creaking old oak table. "Before he makes a mess of my window!"

Pickle quickly opened the door.

"Belch, you old beast, good to see you. You're just in time for dinner."

"My nose has never been treated so well, Hairy Mole, and might I add that you look delightful in your pirate pinny!"

Everybody laughed and welcomed Belch to the table.

"Now, if I am not mistaken, we are one missing." With all the plates full and the gravy slopping over the sides, the pirates drooled as they waited for the final guest. Fingers started to drum, sighs were sighed, watches were tapped and wooden legs STAMPED impatiently on the kitchen floor.

"Well, we might as well st... " began Hairy Mole.

Knock. Knock. Knock.

Hairy got up and strode across the kitchen. He opened the door wide in a theatrical fashion, to prove that this was more than the usual door-opening.

"I am sooooooo sorry I am late, Hairy Mole." Guff the Pirate entered the kitchen and was greeted by several "Where have you beens?" and a couple of "Trust Guffs!" Finally Guff finished her

23

apologies and sat down at the table.

As soon as her pirate bottom found the old oak kitchen chair, the laden forks found their mark and the shovelling commenced.

And without more of a do, the pirates got down to the task of STUFFING their faces.

Three

Trouble Brewing

As the table was cleaned of any trace of food, and the plates and bowls were *thrown* into the sink and quickly washed up, the friends gathered around the old oak kitchen table to listen to Hairy Mole as he began to tell them Toby's story.

"Not so long ago," Hairy began, "the son of my Auntie **Humongous**, Furry Mole, won a trip for one to a faraway island known as **The Crystal Island.**" Hairy Mole looked around the table to make sure his audience was listening.

"It wasn't long before the time had come for Furry to leave. He was to fly by aeroplane to the neighbouring Emerald Island, where he was to take a helicopter that would fly him to the Crystal Island.

"Well, that was the last they saw of him. Not even a postcard or a telephone call. Auntie Humongous has been beside herself with worry. That was over three weeks ago, and we have only just found out what has happened to him, thanks to Toby, who had been doing a bit of wing-warming around the Precious Islands himself. Over to you, Toby."

Hairy Mole turned, newsreader-style, to Toby, who was sitting preening one of his wings.

"Ah, yes, thank you Hairy Mole. Like Hairy Mole has said, I often visit warmer climes for a spot of rest and recuperation, and one of my favourite locations is the Precious Islands. The islands consist of the Emerald Island, the Ruby Island and the island where Furry Mole is currently residing, the Crystal Island.

"When I arrived, as per usual, I found the Precious Islands bathed in glorious sunshine. However, as I looked towards the Crystal Island, my heart was filled with an icy cold fear. The island was under a terrible BLACK CLOUD! I could see *Wild winds*

were whipping up the surrounding sea, creating giant, unsailable waves.

"Anyway, the storms had started the day after Furry's arrival, and they are believed to be the dark doings of three witches: Snot-sprout, Puss-custard and Worm-jelly!" There was a gasp from the group as Toby eyed them one by one with a beady green eye.

"Gaaaaaaaasp!" gasped the pirates.

"These three troublesome hags have been threatening the inhabitants of the Precious Islands for years," Toby continued.

"They appear to have imprisoned all of the islanders of the Crystal Island. This includes not only Hairy Mole's cousin, but also the King and Queen of the whole of the Precious Islands."

"Gaaaaaasssssspppp!" gasped the crew for a second time.

"Fellow pirates," Hairy Mole began. "If we are to attempt to rescue my cousin, it will be a dangerous and strange adventure, with no reward except the heartfelt thanks of my cousin and my Auntie Humongous."

The bold pirates made some shuffling and grunting noises and some slightly sarcastic "Oh good"s and "You couldn't ask for anything more"s.

"However, if we manage to rescue the Royal family of the Precious Islands, they will shower us, I'm sure, with the highest quality royal jam, the like of which no pirate would have ever experienced before."

"Woooooooooooooo hoooooooooooooooooo!"

The kitchen erupted into a din of whoops and cheers as the pirates skipped and danced.

As the high-fives and songs about jam continued, Guff raised her hand in order to ask a question.

"Urrm, Hairy Mole?" Guff started.

"Yes, Guff my girl?" Hairy Mole made himself heard above the noise.

"How do we propose to reach the island if it is surrounded by fierce winds and wild waves?"

The room fell silent and all eyes turned to Hairy Mole.

Hairy Mole's eyes turned to Toby the Seagull.

"A very good question!" Toby replied. The pirates waited in silence for a very good answer.

"Now, Emerald is not only famed for its beautiful coastline and idyllic scenery, it is also well known for the mass of underground caves and tunnels that are rumoured to link the Precious Islands together under the sea. We will use these tunnels!"

"So, treasure and jam, are you with me, men?" Hairy asked his pirates.

"Woooohoooo, yip, yipp!"

"Now, where's the rum?"

The pirates danced and sang way into the night, and it wasn't long before the sun was rising on a new day.

Four

Ready to Go

The **bold** pirate crew were due to leave that afternoon. Toby had given Hairy Mole directions to the Precious Islands and had instructed him to seek out a **Dr Dennison** upon his arrival on Emerald Island.

Dr Dennison owned an old-fashioned shop selling books and charts, maps and compasses. Toby knew that if anyone was able to help them find the tunnels, it would be him.

It wasn't long before Hairy Mole's crew had gone to their homes to collect their baggage, with strict instructions to meet at the dock at five o'clock sharp.

That afternoon, at around five o'clock, T-towel the Cat sat at the kitchen window of Mrs Bulbous Mole's small but well-stocked seaside cottage. On the old oak kitchen table lay a note written by Mrs Bulbous Mole's son, Hairy.

Dear Mother
Have gone to rescue cousin Furry. May not return due to high-risk situation involving witches. If I do return I will bring you treasure and jam, so please keep a space free in the larder (thanks).
If I don't return I have promised my bedroom to T-towel the Cat.
Anyway, hope you are well.
Lots of love,
Hairy
P.S. I have eaten a turkey from your well-stocked larder (thanks).

"Good luck, Hairy Mole," thought T-towel to herself. "I think you're going to need it!"

Five

Feeling Hot Hot Hot!

Hairy Mole and his pirate crew set out that afternoon, a little after six o'clock. Mr Bogey, Pickle, Belch, Crevice, Pit and Guff all took their places on the little ship.

Crevice and Pit pulled in the ropes and unfastened the sails quicker than anyone, thanks to their EXTRA large hands. Pickle, with his EXTREMELY large feet, and Belch, with his EQUALLY big nose, were running up and down the rigging, adjusting pulleys and manoeuvring jibberts, as Mr Bogey stood below, squeaking out instructions to lower this and to be careful with that.

Guff had taken to pouring water into the crow's nest and sitting in it like a bath. This was fine until it became too hot – and then she began to feel like a rabbit in a stew pot.

Hairy Mole stood proudly behind the wheel of the little ship. Toby's map was wedged under his chin as he turned the wheel left a bit, right a bit, and left a bit more.

As the little ship sailed further out to sea, the sun became warmer and fuller in the day, and in the night the stars shone, surrounding the moon as it glowed an unreal, luminous white.

The ship sailed for miles and miles, days and days, nights and nights. The crew became weary and Hairy Mole looked upon them from the wheel of the ship and hoped his calculations were correct. Was it 'left a bit, right a bit' or was it 'left a bit, left a bit more, then right a bit'?

Whichever way it was, it was certainly getting **hotter**. Hairy Mole was currently wearing his special 'cut-down' pirate shorts and a slightly yellowing-around-the-pit-area sleeveless shirt that looked as though it had not only seen better days, but had probably forgotten what those days actually looked like entirely.

Even Mr Bogey had put on his white cricket shirt and trousers to fend off the horrific heat.

There was immense relief when a whoop of joy came from the stew pot – I mean crow's nest – as Guff cried out,

"Whoooooooooooop! Land Ahoy!" Finally, they had

arrived at the first of the Precious Islands, the beautiful Island of Emerald.

Six

Look But Don't Touch

The pirates stood at the side of the little ship and gasped in awe, as the magnificent green sea shimmered and glistened. The whole seabed was encrusted with spectacular shades of green, from emerald to jade, and the fabulous rock formations glittered through the clear water, creating tiny bright-green stars upon the tips of the sun-covered waves.

After "wey-heying" the anchor, the pirates waded through the clear water and sat on the white sandy beach, looking out at the still, shimmering ocean before them.

Not one of them had spoken since leaving the ship, except for the occasional "Wow!" and the odd "Wooo!"

"Quite a sight, isn't it?"
The pirates turned slowly to see who had
spoken to them.

A brown-faced old man stood on the
beach, a few metres away from Hairy Mole and
his crew. The man rubbed his bony fingers
together and twisted his s k i n n y wrists,
until it looked like he would become tangled
and tied together, like a knotted piece of old
rope.

"Oh yes, quite a sight!"
said the man again, this time
twisting his long grey beard into
a tight ball under his chin, so
much so that he had begun to
pull his head down as he
tightened his grip.

"I think it's the most beautiful
sea I have ever seen," said
Hairy Mole, turning his
attention away from the bony
man who, apart from his long
grey beard, was quite naked.

Thankfully the man's beard was quite long enough to cover everything down to his bony knees. Even so, Hairy Mole and the crew preferred looking out to sea rather than facing the nudey stranger.

"So, have you been here long?" Mr Bogey squeaked in the old man's direction, whilst still keeping his eyes firmly fixed on the shimmering sea.

Suddenly, the man opened a sack by his side and scattered some black rocks onto the white sand.

"Oh no, you can't touch them!" The bony man jumped to his feet and started to kick the white sand up into the air, laughing hysterically, his long grey beard flipping and flapping like a giant, hairy, kipper tie.

Quick as a *flash* he was off, running back up the beach, baring his little bony bottom for the entire world to see, until finally he was out of sight.

"What was all that about?" Belch asked

nobody in particular. Getting to his feet, Belch strode over to the black rocks, his giant medallion swaying like a pendulum on a clock, as he bent down, picked one up and held it to his cavernous nostrils.

"It smells like ... well, like sprouts actually!" Belch nodded to himself and passed the rock around the ring of inquisitive pirates.

Hairy Mole raised a questioning eyebrow and sniffed the rock himself.

"Snniiiiiiiiiiiiiifffffff"

sniffed Hairy Mole, his nostril hairs quivering as he inhaled. It appeared to be quite true; the nudey man's black rocks smelt just like sprouts. None of the pirates knew what to make of their situation, and after much discussion they picked up the small sprout rocks and put them into Guff's rucksack.

A pathway at the edge of the white sandy beach led the pirates through some woods and into a clearing. At the centre of the clearing was a large wooden post. Upon the post were four signs, pointing to four different paths. The path from where they had just come read Emerald Cove ⟩.

"We must have just come from Emerald Cove," squealed Mr Bogey with excitement.

"Yes," Hairy Mole wearily agreed, and read out the other three signs:

⟨ Emerald Castle   Crystal Port ⟩

⟨ Emerald Shop-arama

"Where do you think we should head for, Hairy Mole?" Mr Bogey and the crew turned to their captain, eagerly anticipating his answer. Hairy Mole sighed to himself.

"Well, Dr Dennison owns a shop, so which one do you think we should choose?" Hairy Mole asked, raising a big bushy eyebrow.

"Oh, let's go to the castle!" shouted the twins.

"What about the port? I bet the doctor loves a good port," suggested Pickle.

"What about ... "

"We're going this way!" shouted Hairy Mole, stomping off in the direction of the sign pointing to the Emerald shops.

"Good idea, Captain." Everyone heartily agreed and followed Hairy Mole down the well-trodden path towards the shops.

Seven

Dr Dennison

After a few moments and a close shave with a falling coconut, Hairy Mole and his crew wandered out of the palm tree forest and into a bright and breezy little village green.

The village green was surrounded by lots of shops, and several people were busily going about their business, making sure they ignored the odd-looking strangers that had just appeared from the undergrowth.

After a few unsuccessful attempts at asking for directions to Dr Dennison's shop, Hairy Mole eventually ordered his crew to split up and report back as soon as they'd found it for themselves.

"It should have a sign above the door, I'd imagine," said Hairy Mole, scratching his chin.

"What, like 'Dr Dennison's Outrageous Antiquities'?" squeaked Mr Bogey.

"Yes, something like that, Mr Bogey." Hairy Mole laughed at such an idea.

"What, like the sign above your head?" said Guff quietly.

"Yes, like the sign above my ... " Hairy Mole looked above his head and read the sign.

Dr Dennison's Outrageous Antiquities

"That would be that, then," coughed Hairy Mole, before clearing his throat and knocking on the shop door.

"Who is it?" called out a voice.

"We seek Dr Dennison," said Hairy Mole importantly.

"What for?" said the voice.

"Urm, we're looking for a map to get to Crystal Island, so we can defeat some witches and rescue my cousin Furry Mole." Hairy Mole held his hands behind his back and waited.

"Well, why didn't you say so? Come in! Come in!" The door opened and out stepped a dark-looking figure with flared nostrils and the biggest, bushiest pair of eyebrows that you've ever seen in your life.

The fearsome brows looked like two gigantic hairy caterpillars had crawled onto Dr Dennison's face and settled quite happily above both of his eyes.

"Blimey!" whispered Crevice and Pit together.

"Ahem, Dr Dennison, I presume!" Hairy Mole coughed politely.

Inside Dr Dennison's store it smelled musty and old, as though years and years of stories,

maps and charts had been kept secretly hidden away from prying eyes.

Everywhere the crew looked there were shelves filled with books, rolled-up maps, dusty-looking globes and old-fashioned lanterns hanging from the ceiling.

Belch took in a deep sniff:

"Sniiiiiiiiiiiiiiiiiiiiiff."

and was transported to a world where nothing had been discovered and the seas were still full of monsters and adventure.

Dr Dennison invited Hairy Mole and the crew to sit down at a large brass table that was fashioned in the shape of a compass and was as thick as a loaf of bread (probably granary).

While the crew looked around at the wonderful higgledy-piggledy room, Dr Dennison rummaged through a massive wooden box that was full to the brim with rolled-up maps.

After a bit of a delve, the bushy eyebrowed doctor produced a huge map that he unrolled and spread out on the table.

The map was covered in lines and arrows, and drawings of underground caves and tunnels.

Hairy Mole listened carefully as Dr Dennison told him which path he needed to follow to get under the ground from Emerald Island to Crystal Island.

The doctor warned the crew that their

mission to rescue Furry Mole was going to be full of danger and was probably going to include more than a suggestion of mysterious magic and mutated monsters.

The crew shivered at the thought of what lay ahead, but they bravely puffed out their chests when Dr Dennison reminded them that the whole of the Precious Islands were counting on them to defeat the evil witches.

After a nice cup of tea and a bit of a chit-chat, Hairy Mole thanked Dr Dennison for the map and got up to leave.

"Wait!" said Dr Dennison, as he dived into a large suitcase that was bursting with strange objects.

Hairy Mole and the crew waited patiently by the door, until finally Dr Dennison pulled out an old antique pocket watch and handed it to Hairy Mole.

"Take this, brave pirate," he said with a bow.

"Well, thanks very m ... " Hairy Mole was cut short.

"That watch quite possibly belonged to Blackbeard's first mate's best friend's brother. And not only that, it tells the time, sea mileage and ... " Dr Dennison paused.

"Yes?" Hairy Mole asked quietly.

"It glows in the dark!" Dr Dennison growled.

Eight

Tactical Changes

At that very moment, from the top of a tall, thin grey stone tower, Hairy Mole's cousin Furry Mole let out a long s i g h .

"Huuuuuuuuuuuuuuuuuuuuuuuhhh!"

sighed Furry Mole.

Furry had been sitting in the same damp and cold prison cell for over three weeks, and was as bored as a badger in a bathtub.

The prison was tiny and Furry had got used to sitting and staring miserably out of the little b a r r e d window, as black clouds, lightning and thunder rumbled away in the distance.

The only things that kept Furry Mole

amused were the twice-daily games of cockroach football – those and the large roast dinners that would appear up to three times a day, just out of thin air.

The football games had originally started with Furry Mole flicking a small stone into a crowd of cockroaches. To his surprise the roaches had responded, slowly at first but then with more passion.

As the cockroach skills improved, Furry scratched a couple of goals on opposite walls of the cell and organised two teams, with eleven cockroaches on each side.

It was a bit dull at first, as none of the cockroaches knew what to do and simply scuttled about, clicking their legs and waving their long antennae.

However, slowly, after some coaxing, the cockroaches had begun to respond to Furry's positioning and instructions, and had even started to train and play amongst themselves when Furry was asleep.

stone wall staring
window. Then

"P

The roaches practised heading and taking corners, penalties and shooting, passing and dribbling, and it wasn't long before they would troop out from the dark, gloomy corners of the little prison cell ready to take their positions on the pitch.

Furry Mole whistled and clapped as great moments of skill and six-footed challenges took place before his very eyes.

Even though the cockroaches provided entertainment, it was inevitable that Furry now found himself sitting against the cold

out of the small, barred
, suddenly ...

SSSSSSSSSSSSSSSSSSttt!"

Furry sat up abruptly. Had he imagined
that voice? Was it just in his head, or had the
cockroaches started to play tricks on him?
(Why, that cheeky Rooney roach!)

"I say!" said the voice again, "is anybody
there?"

Furry crept across to the tiny grate in the
floor and whispered back, "Hello, I am here!"

"Oh gosh, this is fantastic. Thank my **lucky pants** there is someone else in this horrible prison. I heard you cheering and thought you sounded happy enough. I don't suppose you've found a way out, have you?" said the voice through the grate.

"Unfortunately not. All that happens in my little cell is cockroach football and magic chickens!" laughed Furry Mole, slightly hysterically.

"Magic chickens?" said the rather amazed voice.

"Yes, magic roast chicken dinners. They sort of appear on a big plate and taste delicious. I usually eat them and then watch the match."

"And this would be a cockroach football match, yes?" asked the voice.

"Yes, that's right. Good old cockroach footy!" Furry Mole laughed again.

"Have you been here long?" asked the voice.

Nine

Magic Chickens

Furry Mole sat staring into the brass grate on his cell floor. He had been trapped for over three weeks, but this was the first time he had heard another voice – apart from the furious clicking of the cockroaches, especially after a hotly disputed offside decision.

Even the food that appeared by magic would just disappear the same way, without even a "Can I take your plate?" or a "How was your meal?"

The food was always the same: roast chicken and vegetables, which was actually Furry Mole's favourite meal.

At first he had been scared of the magic chicken. But as his stomach had begun to rumble loudly with hunger, he had started to look forward to the roast chickens' appearances, and was always left wanting more.

Furry Mole even found himself putting on a bit of weight, but every time the food arrived he would eagerly wolf it down and still feel worryingly hungry for more.

"Hello, are you still there? Please say you're still there!" the voice from the grate called again.

"I'm still here, voice," said Furry Mole.

"My name is Furry Mole. I won a trip to the Precious Islands on the back of a Pirate Booty cereal packet." Furry sat cross-legged with his head in his hands, staring at the grate.

"Well, Furry, I have some bad news for you. Beautiful Crystal Island has been captured by three terrible witches. They are determined to steal every last one of our precious gems, until we are left with nothing but rock."

"What do witches want with precious gems?" Furry Mole scratched his head.

"They want to use them to make themselves

stronger, so they'll be powerful enough to take over the whole world! I've seen them greedily crushing crystals in a giant cauldron far beneath the ground. They are trying to produce six huge gems, one to put over each of their eyes. When this is done they'll have enough power to cause all sorts of trouble."

"How do you know all this?" Furry stared at the grate.

"I know this, Furry, because I am the King of the Precious Islands, and we don't have long left before all six giant-sized crystals are created. And then it will be too late!"

"Gosh. Hello Your Majesty! Do you have a plan?" said Furry Mole.

"Your guess is as good as mine, Furry, and don't worry about that 'Majesty' malarkey. Just call me Peter."

Furry scratched his head and furrowed his brow. If a King couldn't escape, what chance did *he* have?

Ten

Beauty and the Beast

Underneath the raging seas surrounding Crystal Island, Hairy Mole and his crew followed Dr Dennison's map and crept silently through dark t u n n e l s and cool, damp caves.

Pickle held an old lantern above his head and the others picked their way over the slippery rocks, as they followed the flickering flame.

Hairy Mole tried his best to study the map by the light of the lantern.

Mr Bogey peered over Hairy Mole's shoulder and squinted, as he tried to look at the directions.

Guff followed along at the back and was more scared of Belch's large bottom than of anything else that might appear out of the darkness.

As the pirates walked through the tunnels, they began to feel more damp and slimy, and it wasn't long before slippy gloop was dripping off the walls and onto their clothes.

"It's like walking through a giant nostril," whispered Belch.

"Nostril, nostril, nostril ... " Belch's voice echoed around the tunnel walls.

"SSSSShhhhh," sssssshhh'd Hairy Mole.

"SSSSShhhhh, SSSSShhhhh, SSSSShhhhh."

"Sorry," whispered Belch.

"Sorry, sorry, sorry ... "

Suddenly Pickle stopped, and the light of the lantern formed seven giant flickering shadows. In front of Pickle was a small wooden door in the rocks. Slowly, Pickle tried the brass handle. The door opened with a loud creak.

'Creeeeeeeeeeeeeeeeeeeeeeaaaa aaaaaaaaaaakkkkkkkkkkkk!'

One by one the crew walked through the door and into a gigantic underground chamber.

"Oh my!" squeaked Mr Bogey.

The whole chamber had been carved out of the rock. The walls, floor and ceiling were twinkling, winking and blinking with crystals.

The pirates ran in different directions to touch the precious stones and laugh at their distorted reflections.

Guff stared at a wall that shimmered and shined and reflected the rest of the crew, as they danced and shook their heads in amazement.

She could see Hairy Mole's hat, as he waved it in the air in celebration.

She could see Belch's medallion bouncing off his chest, as he jigged from one foot to another.

 Then Guff saw a pair of flashing red eyes.

Then Guff saw a pair of large, black, hairy paws.

 Then Guff saw a set of sharp teeth that oozed green goo.

Finally, Guff saw the body of a huge slimy monster that had crept from a dark hole in the side of the chamber.

"AAAAAAArrrrrrgggggggghhhhhhhhh!!!!" screamed Guff, as she watched the slippery beast stand on its hind legs and start to walk towards Mr Bogey.

The monster raised its giant clawed paws above its head and snarled its large sharp teeth, just beside Mr Bogey's right ear.

"EEEEEEEEEEEkkkkkkkkkkk!"

"EEEEEE squeaked Mr Bogey, in a voice even shriller than usual.

Guff and the rest of the crew ran to one of three small, dark caves at the side of the crystal cavern, but poor Mr Bogey had got left behind!

"ROOOOOOOOOOOOOOOOO ooaaaaaaaaaaaaaaaaa aaaaaaarrrrrrrrrrrrrrr!"

roared the slime monster.

"Run, Mr Bogey, ruuuun!" yelled Guff.

Mr Bogey didn't need a second chance. He ran as fast as his cricket bat would allow him.

STAMP tink,
STAMP tink,
STAMP tink.

Just as the monster was about to bite Mr Bogey, the one-legged pirate threw himself across the shiny floor and slid all the way to where the rest of the crew were hiding.

Mr Bogey smashed into the huddle of pirates, sending them flying like skittles, head-first into the darkness of the little cave where they'd been hiding.

"Woooooooooooooooooooooopppps!"

yelled the crew, as they began to slide down a slippery slope, down, down, down and away from the monster – but into what lay ahead, they did not know.

The slime-covered pirates picked themselves up and, after a check to see if anything was broken, they all slowly raised their eyes skywards.

A crack of lightning lit up the hole above them and there they

saw the silhouettes of several dark figures
staring in through the open roof.

"Hello there," called down an extremely
posh, un-monster-like voice. "Do you
chaps need a hand?"

"Urrm, yes please," Hairy Mole
managed to call out.

With that, the posh monster dropped
    a rope
  ladder
  down
    the
  side
of the slimy wall. Slowly, the pirates climbed
the ladder.

Eventually Hairy Mole and his bold pirate crew
reached the top and stood in the pouring rain,
surrounded by their rescuers.

Eleven

A New Diet

"Ping!"

Another plate of food appeared in front of Furry Mole. The vegetables were piled high around the tender white chicken. This was the fourth plate that day, and Furry rubbed his oversized belly and began to tuck in, as though he hadn't eaten for months.

"Furry, are you there?" The King's voice echoed through the grate, making Furry drop one of his sprouts on the floor.

"I have something to say, Furry, and I don't

think you are going to like it!"

Furry finally put down his fork and listened to the King.

"I'm pretty sure those three hags are planning to get you as juicy as a giant tomato before they eventually eat you, possibly as a main meal, maybe as some sort of cold buffet. I'm not sure about the facts, but for the love of yourself, STOP EATING!"

"Eat me?" Furry squeaked.

"How are you looking weight-wise?" the King asked.

Furry looked down at his expanded belly. He felt like a stuffed pillow – but twice as comfy.

"I can't help it, the food is so delicious and I'm the size of an over-inflated beach ball. Do you really think they want to eat me?" Furry began to p u s h the plate away.

"Well I don't think those crones do anything out of kindness. You must resist, Furry Mole."

Furry pushed the plate further away and watched as the cockroaches eagerly tucked into the food.

It was all that he could do to try and stop himself from crying. He stared out of the window, as the clicking and burping cockroaches devoured every last morsel of roast chicken dinner.

'Clickclickburpburp.'

Twelve

Strong Hearts

Captain Francis Tastic had been the leader of the Precious Islands' Special Forces for just over ten years. He had fought in several battles defending the islands, including: the Battle of the Rock, the Battle of the Hill and (not forgetting) the Battle of the Badger.

The last battle being particularly hard-fought due to some particularly tough demands made by the badger regarding broccoli, pizza and flapjacks.

But these were nothing compared to what he now had to face against the three witches: Puss-custard, Worm-jelly and Snot-sprout.

Captain Tastic raised his hand in the air, ordering the men following him to stop. Francis's *immaculate moustache* twitched ever so slightly as the men piled into each other. The band of men that followed Captain Tastic were six of his best soldiers. They had escaped with him after the witches had trapped them in one of the dungeons at the Crystal Castle.

There were also a further seven men who were wearing pirate costumes and appeared to be covered in green slime. Francis thought that these 'new' men appeared to be a bit of a rag-tAg crowd, especially the one with the cricket bat for a leg. Come to think of it, they all looked a bit dodgy!

"Right men," Captain Tastic began.

"Some days are better than others. Some days you face a challenge and some days the challenges that you face need bravery and a strong heart. This, my friends, is one of those days."

A thunderous roar was heard from up above, as a gigantic burst of thunder boomed and a flash of lightning split the dark sky.

"I propose we walk up this hill and attempt to seize control of the tall tower at the top of it. Once we've seized control, we'll have a look for something else to seize. Are you with me?" shouted Francis, above the noise of the rain.

"Yes sir!" called back the soldiers.

"Blimey!" Belch whispered to Pickle, "I don't know about a strong heart, but I'm going to need a strong stomach if there are any more speeches like this!"

As Francis continued to tell the small group how he intended to seize more things in order to rescue the King, Hairy Mole the Pirate stood listening to the speech. The strength of the Captain's voice, the way he stood: this man, thought Hairy Mole, could move mountains if he had a jolly good reason to do it.

Then Hairy began to listen to a low whisper coming from one of his pirates.

"What a load of poop! Here we are, standing in the rain, and this Hairy Mary is droning on about the importance of this and the strength of that. I prefer a good old Hairy Mole speech. No words, just action!"

Hairy Mole smiled to himself, as his crew and Captain Tastic's soldiers slowly started to wind their way up the slippery and muddy hill towards the tall tower at the top.

Thirteen

HELP!

In the tower on the hill, Furry Mole was hopping excitedly from one foot to another. He had watched the group of figures approaching the large wooden doorway, far down below his little barred window. Now it looked as though, at last, he might be rescued.

Furry called out to the King in delight, as the small group of men stood below him, scratching their heads and generally looking indecisive.

"They're going to try to enter the tower. We're going to be saved, King, saved I tell you!" Furry skipped over to the grate and put his ear to the floor. The only response from the grate was the sound of the wind blowing through the old tower.

The King was gone.

Down in the witches' cave, the eyes of Worm-jelly and Puss-custard, magnified by their watermelon-sized jewels, sparkled with evil as they stood over King Peter of the Precious Islands.

Snot-sprout poked the King with her pointy stick.

"Where are the rest of the crystals, you old fool?" Snot-sprout looked even more peculiar than usual, as she only had one giant crystal over her left eye.

The tired King looked at the witch and answered with nothing but silence.

"Right then, King Stupid. I may have a little something that will make you change your mind!"

An almighty burst of light exploded from high above their heads. The King gasped in horror as he watched a glowing, shimmering bubble float down from the roof of the cave. Inside the see-through sphere, the Queen of the Precious Islands pressed her hands against the sides and screamed a noiseless scream, as she slowly floated down towards her husband and the horrible witches.

"So then, King! What's it to be?" cackled Puss-custard.

The King of the Precious Islands placed his head in his hands and wept, as the Queen hung inside the ball suspended above his head.

"Do I have any choice, you vicious crones?" the King shouted with rage. Then, proudly and with dignity, he stood up and announced: "Release the Queen and I will show you where to find the Crystal Cavern!"

High above, inside the floating ball, the Queen of the Precious Islands screamed a silent scream, as she watched her husband lead the three dancing witches out of the cave and down towards the gem-encrusted cavern below.

Fourteen

Now I've Seen Everything!

Thuuuuuuuump. The sound of wood on wood echoed around the base of the tower, as the pirates and soldiers tried again to break through the thick, oak door. They were using an old fallen oak tree as a battering ram. The base of the trunk was still charcoal-black and smouldering from where it had been hit by lightning, and the group struggled with the weight as, yet again, they tried to break down the door.

Thuuuuuuuump.

As Hairy Mole stood at the front of the tower, looking towards the heavens, he suddenly felt something land on his head. Then there was another 'something', and another, and another, until finally Hairy Mole found himself running for cover, just in case a

larger 'something' fell on his head and squashed him flat.

Then the 'somethings' stopped falling from the sky and Hairy looked at the ground in front of him to see what they actually were.

Hairy Mole stood in amazement as shiny and particularly plump little black cockroaches danced around on the muddy ground before him. Slowly but surely, the little creatures began to spell out a word ...

H ... E ... L ...

"AAAArrrrrrgggggghhhhhh!"

screamed the pirate at the thought of the next letter. Then he managed to contain himself and continued to watch 'P' appear before his eyes.

"H.E.L.P. – Help!" shouted Hairy Mole excitedly. The men all looked upwards to see where the amazing FAT beetle word had come from. High above their heads they could see a little white shirt being waved from a tiny barred window.

"My goodness, that's Furry!"
cried out Hairy Mole with joy. "If we could just get through those doors."

Hairy ran as fast as he could, straight at the solid oak door.

'Booooooooooooooooooiiinnnggggggggg!'

Hairy Mole bounced off the door, straight onto Captain Tastic.

Francis Tastic squealed as Hairy Mole put his large pirate boot squarely on Francis's patent leather soldier's shoe.

"AAAArrrrrgggggghhhhhh!" screamed Captain Tastic, hopping around on one leg.

Belch dodged out of the way and crashed right into Pickle, who fell over backwards waving his arms in the air, as he fell onto the piece of wood that was balanced with Guff at the other end.

"Woooooooooooooooooooooop!"

Guff yelled, as she found herself catapulted high into the sky. Up and up she flew, past the old oak door, past Furry Mole's little barred window, until finally she landed on the flat roof of the tower.

Looking around, Guff suddenly spied an open door with some stone steps leading downwards.

"I wonder ... " Guff wondered to herself.

Furry Mole too stared out of his window, waiting for the flying pirate to pass again, this time downwards. But suddenly there was a knock at the door.

"Hello?" he whispered nervously.

"Is that Furry Mole, cousin of Hairy Mole the Pirate?" the voice asked.

"Yes it is. Who am I talking to?" asked Furry, relieved that the voice sounded friendly, if not a little out of breath.

"I am Guff the Pirate and to be honest with you I have just flown past your window and I am slightly disturbed by the whole flying experience. However, there seems to be a key here, so if you wait for one moment ... "

Slowly the key turned in the lock, and then, for the first time in weeks, Furry Mole was greeted by a face other than that of a football-playing cockroach.

The face was covered in mud and green slime, but Furry Mole hugged little Guff with all his might, before waving goodbye to his ever-growing football team and slamming the cell door shut behind him.

Fifteen

Good Luck

From All the Boys

When Hairy Mole saw Furry he ju^mp_ed in the air and clicked his heels together.

The two cousins hugged each other as the rain poured onto their heads, and Guff was treated to hearty pats on the back from the rest of the crew.

"Yes, yes, an amazing act of bravery," bellowed Hairy Mole, after finally releasing his cousin from a vice-like bear hug. "Guff you are

indeed a hero and we are all **very** proud!"
Hairy Mole gripped Guff on both shoulders
and kissed her squarely on the forehead.

"Oooww!" cried Guff, as Hairy Mole's
stubbly chin scratched her nose.

Everybody was in jubilant mood and even
the cockroaches, despite the rain, had managed
to spell out a message to their friend and
footballing mentor:

GOOD LUCK BOSS, FROM ALL THE BOYS!

Furry was overcome with emotion and
wiped a tear from his eye, before bidding his
team farewell as they clicked off back to the
dark cell to eat some more of that delicious
magic chicken.

Furry turned to the rest of the group.

"We still have a lot to do, I'm afraid. When
I was trapped in the tower I made contact with
the King of the Precious Islands."

"The King is alive?" shouted Francis.

The soldiers and pirates eagerly crowded around Furry Mole, as he told them what had happened.

Captain Tastic listened in horror as Furry told how the King had recently disappeared and how they had hardly any time left until the witches would have enough crystals to carry out their **dastardly scheme.**

"If I'm not mistaken," squeaked a very damp Mr Bogey, "there can be only one place on the Precious Islands where those horrible hags will be found!"

As a bolt of lightning shot out of the sky, lighting up their muddy faces, the group cried out,

"The Crystal Cavern?"

"Oh, I was actually thinking of that nice little crystal shop next to Dr Dennison's store on Emerald Island. But, yes, to the Crystal Cavern!" Mr Bogey shouted, as he raised his arm high in the air.

Sixteen

"Mine, all Mine!"

"OOOOOOOOhhhhhhh!"

"AAAAAAAAhhhhhhhhh!"

"Mmmmmmmmmmmmmm!"

The three witches blinked their crystal-covered eyes as the King led them down into the beautiful Crystal Cavern.

"Mine, all mine!" Snot-sprout screamed horribly.

The King looked on in disgust as the witches filled their pockets with shining stones.

"Release the Queen, you disgusting hags, you have what you want." The King fought back tears as the witches continued to rip crystals from every part of the cavern.

"What right do you have to tell us to do anything, you stupid little King?" asked Snot-sprout.

"You gave me your word!" the King yelled.

Snot-sprout grabbed her potbelly from laughing so much and she threw back her bony head and screamed with delight.

"Haaaaaaahaaaaaaaheeeeeeheeeeee, 'you gave me your word!'"

As Snot-sprout continued to laugh, she felt a blast of smelly, hot breath on her shoulder.

"Phew!" she declared, "one of you two has got to cut down on the fish eyes and kitten noses, because your breath Steeeeeeeeinks!"

Snot-sprout spun round to see which witch it was, blowing their smelly breath in her direction.

"GGGGGGGGGRRRRRrrrrrrrrrrrrrrr!"

The beast **oozed** green goo from the sharp corners of its mouth as it padded, hairy paw after hairy paw, towards the frightened crone.

The long, hairy snout of the slimy beast was almost touching the long warty nose of Snot-sprout as she stumbled backwards, almost tripping over herself to escape the foul-smelling creature.

As Snot-sprout looked over her shoulder, she saw the King standing with his arms crossed, staring right at her.

"Release the Queen!"

cried the King.

"GGGGGrrrrrrr!" growled the

slimy beast, as Worm-jelly and Puss-custard edged their way back towards the passage that led to their lair.

They stopped suddenly as Snot-sprout screamed out to them.

"SISTERS, release the Queen! For the love of me, release the Queen!"

The beast had placed one razor-sharp claw under the wobbling chin of the cowering crone and was now carefully caressing a particularly fat wart.

Worm-jelly and Puss-custard turned around and ran, with crystals spilling from their pockets and tinkling onto the ground.

The sound of the crystals being stolen diverted the beast's attention and it stared with sad eyes as the thieves fled the cavern.

A split-second was all it took for Snot-sprout to overcome her fear and, clutching her pointing stick in her tightly clenched fist, she created a spark that flashed a bright light directly into the sad, red eyes of the beast.

The creature lumbered backwards, temporarily blinded, as Snot-sprout scurried after her sisters with her pockets bulging full of crystals.

All that could be heard were the distant echoes of cackling laughter, as the three witches disappeared down the tunnel and back towards their lair.

Seventeen

In a Hole

High up above the caves and caverns under Crystal Island, the rain continued to pour, pummelling the soldiers and pirates until they were sopping wet and ever so slightly irritable.

Hairy Mole leaned into the wind, as its sheer force tried to push him off his feet and on to his hairy bottom.

Next to Hairy Mole, Captain Francis Tastic vainly fought the elements. His once-perfect moustache had been turned upside down by the diabolical weather, so he looked like he had a very large waxed smile upon his chiselled face.

"Can I be honest with you, Hairy Mole?" Francis turned to the pirate, shouting over the noise of the wind. "I'm not entirely sure where we are gooooooooiiiiiiiiiiinnnnnggg..."

"What?" Hairy shouted, turning to the Captain, who had vanished into thin air.

"What is it Hairy Mole?" squeaked Mr Bogey.

"W-w-witches!" stammered Hairy Mole. "The witches have vanished Captain Tastic!"

"Oi, I'm down here!" called a tiny voice. "It's me, Francis. I'm down here!"

Just as a crack of lightning lit up the entire island, there was Captain Francis Tastic's head, covered in mud and talking from down on the ground.

"Oh my goodness, the witches have vanished his body and left just a head. How hideous!" Mr Bogey looked ready to explode with anger, and was already lining up his bat with a nearby tree.

One of the biggest, GRUFFEST soldiers flung himself to the ground in floods of tears.

"Oh sir, how could they do this to you? How will you be able to live a normal life just as a head?" The soldier, whose name was Perkins, grabbed the head between both hands and held it tightly to his muddy bosom.

"Get off me, Perkins, you big girl's blouse. **I've fallen down a hole!** Nothing to do with witches. Now get me out of here, before I really give you something to cry about!"

"It looks to me like you have got two choices," said Furry, bending down to the Captain's head. "We can either push you or pull you." Furry stood up and looked at Perkins.

"Let's grab his ears!"

Perkins almost had a smile on his face as he reached down to the talking head.

"PUSH ME, PUSH ME!" screamed Francis.

"Alright then," grinned Perkins, and clenching an almighty fist he began to clump Captain Francis Tastic's head right into the ground, just as if he were hammering a nail into a plank of wood.

It only took a couple of whumps and the head disappeared.

'Whuuump!'

'Whuuump!'

"AAAArrrrgggghhhhh!"

screamed Francis, as he found himself plunging into darkness and hurtling in a decidedly downwards direction.

"Oooops!" said Perkins.

Eighteen

"They've Got Our Lunch!"

"What was that screaming noise?" Snot-sprout's beady eye looked towards the entrance of their cave.

"Nothing, sister. Come and empty your pockets. We have more than enough horrible crystals to give you the final giant eye. Then the whole of the world will be ours."

The sisters eagerly surrounded the large black cauldron that was, by now, overflowing with crystals.

Snot-sprout stirred in the gems with her poking stick, shrieking with laughter as finally the last, fabulous giant crystal began to rise from the depths of the black pot.

Snot-sprout raised the oversized

crystal in the air, as if she were holding aloft a new-born baby, before turning jubilantly to her sisters, her black teeth grinning in triumph.

"Stop that you wicked, wicked witch!" commanded an authoritative voice.

Snot-sprout looked up to see **King Peter Precious** with another man who had an upturned moustache and a rather large black eye.

As the King and the Captain walked towards the three sisters, it became clear that there were more people coming out of the shadows.

There was a dirty-looking pirate with a hairy mole on his cheek, another pirate with a cricket bat for a leg and a further five decidedly filthy-looking pirates walking into the witches' lair.

"What's all this, King? Fancy dress without the fancy?" Snot-sprout laughed at her own joke as Puss-custard and Worm-jelly stood either side of her.

"We have come to reclaim what rightfully belongs to the Precious Islands." The King pointed to the crystals that lay scattered around the cauldron.

"You and whose army, King?" shouted Puss-custard, spitting yellow phlegm onto the ground.

"Well, mine, actually." Captain Tastic waved a bruised arm and Perkins and the rest of the soldiers stepped into view.

"Hey, they've got our lunch!" Worm-jelly pointed a bony arm at Furry Mole, who blushed ever so slightly.

"Just you be careful, King. Don't you forget about Queenie!" Snot-sprout turned her pointing stick to the bubble floating above them.

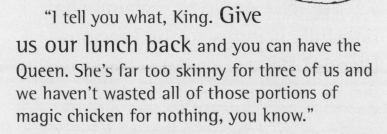

"Queen Tina!" Perkins dropped to his giant knees.

"I tell you what, King. Give us our lunch back and you can have the Queen. She's far too skinny for three of us and we haven't wasted all of those portions of magic chicken for nothing, you know."

Furry blushed even harder and felt embarrassed that he, a young cousin of a pirate, could be seen as a fair swap for the Queen of all the Precious Islands.

"Furry, noooooo!"

It was too late. Furry ran from the group and stopped just out of reach of the witches, his oversized belly wobbling temptingly.

"Take me, if I am worth nothing other than food, take me and release the Queen."

"Deal!" cackled Snot-sprout.

"I feel like pirate tonight, pirate tonight!" she sang happily.

The bubble containing Queen Tina floated gently to the ground and burst, releasing the first lady of the Precious Islands onto her royal behind.

"You horrible creatures, don't you eat that poor pirate!" shouted the Queen.

"A deal's a deal, your Majesty." Furry stepped within Snot-sprout's reach, just as she placed the final giant crystal onto her eyeball.

"That's right, your Majesty, a deal's a deal!" laughed the greedy witches.

Snot-sprout, Puss-custard and Worm-jelly stood on separate sides of the cauldron. The six giant crystals shimmered and shined, as a bolt of lightning shot out of the cauldron and streaked through the air and out into the night sky.

"Chaaaaaarrrrge!" Captain Tastic led from the front, running, sword unsheathed, towards the evil hags.

"Get away from our dinner, you tin-pot soldiers!" Snot-sprout barely turned to look at the Captain as she raised her pointing stick, causing Francis and his soldiers to fall to the floor.

"Not bad, eh?" Snot-sprout winked a magnified eyeball at her sisters, impressed at the sight of her own power.

"Enough is enough!" The King bellowed and ran

towards the cauldron, his white beard flying over his shoulder.

Puss-custard raised her warty hands into the air and suddenly a green light filled the cave, with such force that the King and the Queen fell to the ground, shielding their eyes.

"Who's next eh, pirates? I wonder – will it be the two pip-squeaks at the back?"

Crevice and Pitt frowned.

"What about the two OAFS behind them?"

Pickle and Belch gritted their teeth and growled.

"How about the one with the big ears, or the one with the wooden leg?"

Guff and Mr Bogey clenched their fists ready for action.

"How about the one with the big nostrils and smelly bottom, you twisted sisters?"

Hairy Mole flew through the air, holding his hat over his eyes for protection and making a dive for Furry Mole. Grabbing his cousin, Hairy hoisted him over his back and ran for his life.

"Will you fools never learn?" Snot-sprout stared into the cauldron and summoned up her powers, before pointing her pointy stick over her shoulder.

A beam of green light flew past Hairy Mole's head and towards the rest of the crew.

"Urrrrrp!" gulped Guff, as the light hit Belch straight in the chest.

Nineteen

Help from Above

The beam of light from Snot-sprout's poking stick reflected off Belch's gigantic medallion and shot through the roof of the cave, causing rocks, mud and earth to fall to the cave floor below.

The sisters looked up in terror as not only the roof began to collapse, but something terribly large and heavy came through as well.

"AAAAAAAAAARRRRRGGGGGHHHHHHHHH" they screamed together.

Furry smiled a broad smile as he saw what was coming through the roof. Twenty two gigantic cockroaches fell through the air and crushed the three witches, before they had a chance to shout "beetle blancmange".

The battered and bruised group looked on at the spectacle with a mixture of joy and a slight feeling of nausea, as the crunching and ticking cockroaches fed their ravenous appetites on the three wicked witches.

The Mutated black insects rubbed their hairy arms together as they devoured each sister, until all that remained were six large watermelon-sized crystals and a small, faintly glowing, pointy stick.

The King turned his attention away from the witch banquet and declared, "Now for a feast of our own. Look how the clouds are lifting. We shall eat, drink, dance and sing until we can no more. Thank you all, my friends."

As the King wiped tears of joy from his eyes, a bright beam of sunlight cut through the dark clouds and glorious blue sky could be seen through the hole in the cave roof.

Deep in the recesses of Guff's rucksack the dark, sprout-smelling rocks turned into beautiful, twinkling diamonds.

Twenty

A Nice Bit of Trifle

Hairy Mole and his crew blinked in the sunlight as they clung on to the backs of the giant cockroaches. The massive insects clambered back through the hole in the cave roof and deposited our heroes onto a fresh piece of sprouting grass.

With a wink and a wave, the gigantic footballing roaches disappeared back into the ground.

The cockroaches had decided to help protect the crystals against further attempts at theft. They had also become great friends with the slime-dribbling guardian of the Crystal Cavern. As a matter of fact, the ferocious monster, whose actual name was Gavin, had volunteered to referee some of the roaches' football games for them.

Everyone, especially the King and Queen, was delighted by this arrangement, and as all the Crystal Island villagers rejoiced in a huge fiesta, their royal highnesses, Max and Tina Jewel, laid on a splendid banquet for all the heroes of the day.

The King leant back in his HUGE chair (he must have had about five cushions so he could reach).

"Before you leave my land I will give you a very precious gift and let it be known that, from this day forth, anyone who is a friend of Hairy Mole the Pirate is a friend of the Precious Islands."

"Just one thing, Your Majesty." The King stood in front of Hairy Mole, with one royal foot resting in a bowl of jelly.

"I hope you don't find me too rude, but if you don't mind, I and my crew," Hairy looked around the table as his crew looked proudly back at him, "would be more than happy with some of the finest quality jam."

Everyone exploded with cheers and a cracking new song about jam and trifle.

Suddenly everyone was singing and dancing, and it wasn't long before the banquet spilled out onto the streets.

Everybody joined the carnival and

fireworks, as the whole of the island partied and rejoiced in celebration.

Amongst the celebrations Hairy Mole stood and watched his friends, old and new, as they sung and danced.

The two twins, Crevice and Pitt, were hugging each other in joy and happiness.

Mr Bogey was singing a song about cricket to a much amused King and Queen.

Pickle and Belch had sneaked a whole

keg of rum to themselves and were passing it back and forth in between burps and hiccups.

Little **Guff** danced a jig with Francis Tastic and Perkins.

And do you know what Hairy Mole did?

He *smiled* and *smiled* and *smiled*.

The End